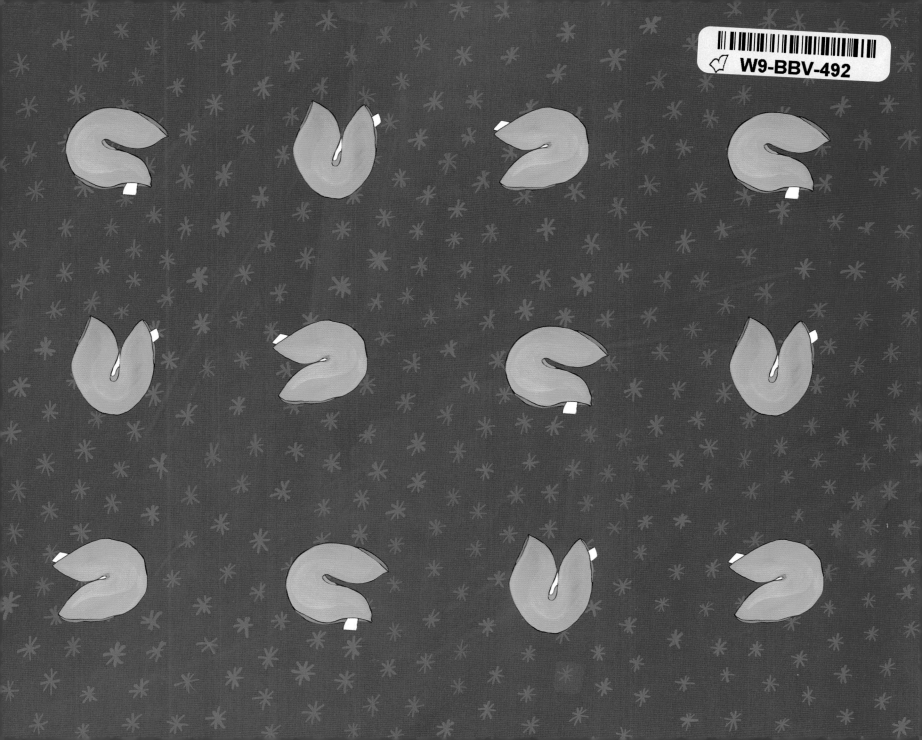

To RISD & Fred Lynch's Fortune Cookie Assignment

THIS IS A BORZOI BOOK PUBLISHED BY ALFRED A. KNOPF
Copyright © 2004 by Grace Lin
All rights reserved under International and
Pan-American Copyright Conventions. Published
in the United States of America by Alfred A. Knopf,
an imprint of Random House Children's Books,
a division of Random House, Inc., New York, and
simultaneously in Canada by Random House of
Canada Limited, Toronto. Distributed by
Random House, Inc., New York.
KNOPF, BORZOI BOOKS, and the colophon are
registered trademarks of Random House, Inc.

www.randomhouse.com/kids

Library of Congress Cataloging in Publication Data
Lin, Grace.
Fortune cookie fortunes / Grace Lin.
p. cm.
SUMMARY: After a young Chinese American girl
opens fortune cookies with her family, she
notices that the fortunes seem to come true.
Includes brief notes on the history of the
fortune cookie.
ISBN 0-375-81521-X (trade)
ISBN 0-375-91521-4 (lib. bdg.)
[1. Fortune cookies—Fiction.
2. Chinese Americans—Fiction.]
I. Title.
PZ7 .L644Fo 2004
[E]—dc21   2003009011

MANUFACTURED IN CHINA
May 2004
10 9 8 7 6 5 4 3 2 1
First Edition

FORTUNE COOKIE FORTUNES

GRACE LIN

ALFRED A. KNOPF
NEW YORK

The best part about eating at a Chinese restaurant is the fortune cookies.
Crack! Crack! Crack!
What will our fortunes say?

Mei-Mei's fortune says:

☺ Your smallest action will attract many.

My fortune says:

☺ You see the world in a different way.

Jie-Jie's fortune says:

☺ Your imagination will create many friends.

"How do you think your fortune will come true, Ba-Ba?" Mei-Mei asks.

"It won't come true," Jie-Jie scoffs. "They never come true."

But I'm not so sure. . . .

The next day, Ba-Ba and I go to the park. "I'm tired," he says, and suddenly I am too. But before I fall asleep, I remember Ba-Ba's fortune:

Your moods are contagious.

When I get back, I go see Ma-Ma.
"The garden is growing so well,"
Ma-Ma says. "It must be the
new fertilizer I'm using."
But her fortune was . . .

☺ Attention and care will make great things happen.

I peek into Jie-Jie's room.
What is she doing?

☺ Your imagination will create many friends.

Then I watch
Mei-Mei refill the
bird feeder. . . .

Your smallest action will attract many.

Everyone's fortune is coming true!
What about mine? Do I see the world
in a different way?

Crows are black everywhere.

You long to travel the world.

Ask a friend to join you on your next voyage.

A train trip might be just the ticket.

You can only succeed if you try.

A thrilling time is in your future.

Sweet fruit sometimes has bruised skin.

You are talented in many ways.

The path of life leads upward.

Patience is a virtue.

Sometimes life goes in circles.

Don't fear the future; you will move quickly.

The important thing is that you express yourself.

The grass is always greener on the other side.

You cannot see if you do not open your eyes.

A blank page has the most potential.

Idleness is the holiday of the fools.

Depart not from the path that fate has assigned you.

You are on the road to your heart's desire.

Your destiny lies before you; choose wisely.

Will I always see the world this way?
There's only one way to find out. . . .

Crack!

Time for another fortune cookie!
What will it say?

☺ Look forward to a life of great fortune!

I think fortune cookie
fortunes are always true,
don't you?

Fortune cookies

Fortune cookies can be considered one of the first true Asian American foods. Associated with Chinese cuisine and Asian culture, the fortune cookie actually originated in the United States in the early 20th century.

The birth of the fortune cookie has many conflicting legends. Most credit David Jung for creating the treat as a promotional device, in 1918, for his Hong Kong Noodle Company in Los Angeles. Others claim that in 1914 a Japanese inventor, Makoto Hagiwara (who intended it as a refreshment at San Francisco's Japanese Tea Garden), introduced the cookie and that local Chinese restaurants seized upon the idea when forced to think of a dessert for tourists.

Fortune cookies do have roots in Chinese culture. The fortune cookie can be seen as a modern reinvention of the moon cake, a round cake eaten at the Mid-Autumn Festival. In the 13th and 14th centuries in China, secret messages were delivered in moon cakes. During the American railway boom in the late 19th century, Chinese workers exchanged biscuits bearing words of encouragement instead of moon cakes at the Mid-Autumn Festival. And thus, the jump to fortune cookies was inevitable.

However, one can trace the fortune cookie to Japanese culture as well. The Japanese New Year custom of receiving good fortunes in a flat, light cracker called a *sembei* can easily be seen as the inspiration for the fortune cookie. The *sembei* is unsweetened, though. Many claim sugar was added to the fortune cookie to appeal to America's sweet tooth.

Regardless, the fortune cookie has been baked into contemporary Asian American culture. Love, wealth, health, luck—all of life's virtues have found themselves imprinted in one shape or form inside the delectable, memorable fortune cookie!

☺